陳秀珍 著
Poems by Chen Hsiu-chen

李魁賢 英譯
Translated by Lee Kuei-shien

簡瑞玲 西譯
Traducido por Chien Jui-ling

保證

Promise
◆
Promesa

陳秀珍漢英西三語詩集
Chinese - English - Spanish

台灣詩叢 • Taiwan Poetry Series 02

【總序】詩推台灣意象

叢書策劃／李魁賢

進入21世紀，台灣詩人更積極走向國際，個人竭盡所能，在詩人朋友熱烈參與支持下，策劃出席過印度、蒙古、古巴、智利、緬甸、孟加拉、馬其頓等國舉辦的國際詩歌節，並編輯《台灣心聲》等多種詩選在各國發行，使台灣詩人心聲透過作品傳佈國際間。接續而來的國際詩歌節邀請愈來愈多，已經有應接不暇的趨向。

多年來進行國際詩交流活動最困擾的問題，莫如臨時編輯帶往國外交流的選集，大都應急處理，不但時間緊迫，且選用作品難免會有不週。因此，興起策劃【台灣詩叢】雙語詩系的念頭。若台灣詩人平常就有雙語詩集出版，隨時可以應用，詩作交流與詩人交誼雙管齊下，更具實際成效，對台灣詩的國際交流活動，當更加順利。

以【台灣】為名，著眼點當然有鑑於台灣文學在國際間名目不彰，台灣詩人能夠有機會在國際努力開拓空間，非為個人建立知名度，而是為推展台灣意象的整體事功，期待開創台灣文學的長久景象，才能奠定寶貴的歷史意義，台灣文學終必在世界文壇上佔有地位。

實際經驗也明顯印證，台灣詩人參與國際詩交流活動，很受重視，帶出去的詩選集也深受歡迎，從近年外國詩人和出版社與本人合作編譯台灣詩選，甚至主動翻譯本人詩集在各國文學雜誌或詩刊發表，進而出版外譯詩集的情況，大為增多，即可充分證明。

承蒙秀威資訊科技公司一本支援詩集出版初衷，慨然接受【台灣詩叢】列入編輯計畫，對台灣詩的國際交流，提供推進力量，希望能有更多各種不同外語的雙語詩集出版，形成進軍國際的集結基地。

2017.02.15誌

目次

*附西班牙語翻譯

冬 2

為了歡迎雪
樹葉
讓出了

整座山

1998

保證

我保證
我敢保證
我用人格用生命向您保證

我們保證
我們敢保證
我們用品格用信譽向您保證

政黨向人民保證
老闆向員工保證
商家向顧客保證
男人向女人保證
女人向小孩保證
蜜蜂向花朵保證
浪花向沙灘保證
風向樹葉保證

愛情向永恆保證
上帝向靈魂保證

保證
保證
保證

血的歷史曾向和平保證

1998

鳥有無限自由

鳥有無限不為人知的自由
鳥有不勞而食的自由
鳥有不擇而棲的自由
鳥有對檻歌唱的自由
鳥有對主人舞蹈的自由
鳥有就地拉屎的自由
鳥有風裡來浪裡去的自由
鳥有近視的自由
鳥有兩腳發軟的自由
鳥有啄掉翅膀的自由
鳥有遺忘愛情的自由
鳥有遺忘敵人的自由
啊啊　鳥
自由
鳥有遺忘自由的自由

1998

洋蔥

剖你的心
流我的淚
愛的難題

1998

夜讀

當夜幕
四垂
我翻開
扉頁
閱讀一首詩
以
唇語

那扉頁　白得十分
澈底
我讀它千遍
萬遍

測得
一首詩的
長度是
一整個　藍透了的

液態的
夏夜

無字的
詩
密密麻麻甜膩膩的你的
名字

1998

閱讀

你細細審閱一枚葉子
那上面有著創世紀吧！

每一條葉脈邁向年輪的奧秘
訴說著歲月的繁華

一片葉子可能導覽一座森林
一座森林可能藏著
開啟世界的密碼

捧讀聖經般
你深深審視
一枚葉子

2003.12.18

潛水事件

我沒入水中
有人喊救命
有人丟下救生圈
有人奮不顧身噗通跳下水
最後他們才發現
我只是在挑戰自己
潛水技能的極限

當我再度落水
有人歡呼加油
有人手持鮮花等候我
啦啦隊裡無人知曉
我已漸漸喪失潛水的能力

2005.06

森林

生命之樹的秋天
記憶就像葉片
逐片泛黃
剝落

穿越森林
遍地彩葉
像一冊冊回憶錄
散開的紙頁

偶然
我拾起一葉
記憶的殘骸

森林一望無際
我無從分辨這一葉
究竟屬於哪一棵哪一枝

總有不願掉落的葉片在風中
像蜘蛛網上的獵物顫動
正在抵抗剛強的消亡

從望斷來時路
到有時忘掉來時路
終至忘斷來時路

一轉身
霧吞沒了整片森林
　　　　　　　　整座記憶

宇宙
重返創世紀

2013.01.24

人與神 1

戰爭的雙方
信仰相同的神

左方堅信　真理站在己方
右方堅信　公義站在己方

雙方同時面向相同的神
祈求同一戰場的勝利

神分裂成兩半
左右為難

2014.07.28

人與神 2

戰爭的雙方
信仰不同的神

雙方各自面向自己的神祈求
同一戰場的勝利

左方堅信己方必勝
右方堅信對方必敗

人與人的戰爭演變成
無辜的
神與神的戰爭

人用砲彈決定
誰的神
才是真神

2014.07.28

銅像 1

連回頭的能力都沒有
銅像站在
人為墊高的基座上
睥睨天下

咀嚼了
數十年的歷史
如今
吐不出一絲記憶的殘渣

目中無人的銅像
迷失在時空錯亂的路口
發呆了多少歲月

站在歷史的轉捩點
銅像是
找不到路的失智老人

2014.08.14

銅像 2

硬
和木乃伊比賽
誰更不朽

銅像與木乃伊
一個躺平
一個還硬撐

一個具有軟實力
在博物館占有
一席之地

一個還
在歷史上
找不到定位

2014.08.20

有機生活

你過你的有機生活
睜開眼第一件事
就是滑手機
滑來滑去
把自己滑到非現實的世界

我過我的無機生活
睜開眼第一件事
就是看到你在滑手機
滑去滑來
把我滑出了你的有機世界

在你有機世界的農場裡
有叫醒心智的公雞嗎？

你過你的有機生活
我過我的無機生活

你睜開眼第一件事
就是滑手機
我睜開眼第一件事
就是看到你在滑手機

滑來滑去
把自己滑到非現實的世界
滑去滑來
把我滑出了你的有機世界

在你有機世界的農場裡
有叫醒公雞的心智嗎？

2014.08.05

面具

彩粧的　面具
再也遮掩不住歲月橫行
的足跡

換一張整型的　面具
讓青春在五官復活
年輪的祕密隱藏軀體

人人搶換明星臉
名醫不停為信眾開光
換一張臉如換一張名片
換一張臉如換一張遮羞布

而我僅僅擁有一張
無法回春的臉
袒然面對天地
五官是自然美展演的舞台

我這張忠實於上帝的臉
考驗
你對我得
愛

2014.11.25

不確定的風景

一朵雲
拖著一整片天空
行走過多少時間

兩顆眼珠
領著一具軀體
行走過多少曠野

這一切
都即將被一張
醉酒的紅臉
熄燈

瞬間成為
不確定的風景

2015.03.06

海 1

海
收藏天空的眼淚
因而流著深藍血液

海
和一座含笑青山遙遙相望
因而染患綠色的相思

在我心中
也藏著一個海洋

隔著一片海域
我和一座永遠不能進入的孤島
遙遙相望

每當我望著天空發問
我的眼睛就忍不住

保證

Promise

向心中的海洋
掉下鹹鹹的眼淚

心中的海洋氾濫時
我就轉向茫茫大海
垂下我的珍珠淚

淚眼灌溉的海洋
會把眼淚
還給天空

2015.07.22

桃花

妳說
沒人喜歡真實桃花
大家都愛上
沒有眼淚的塑膠花

可是
我一直都在
我老早就在
妳身邊

你忙於哭泣的眼睛
就是
看不見我

2015.07.31

心跳聲

時鐘掛在
客廳的心臟地帶
發出
老屋的心跳聲

我不在
你的心臟地帶
卻渴望
發出你的心跳聲

你佔領
我的心臟地帶
卻發出
他人的心跳聲

人子釘在
歷史的心臟地帶

發出
復活的心跳聲

2015.08.08

讀詩

用盛開的耳朵
讀詩

我迷醉
在你微透酒香的神祕顫音
我用你的詩
你的每一句每一個字
紋我的心

我迷失
在你語言曲折的迷宮
我翻閱多少重峻嶺
終於
在山嵐飄渺花香瀰漫的森林中
捕獲白鹿

但你終將遠離的腳步
已經敲亂
敲痛我的心

2015.09.07

門

我的門
是為了讓你打開

魔術師的紅巾下藏著甚麼祕密
神廟裡住著甚麼神

門後隱藏
一片讓你驚呼的風景

衣服
是薄薄的一層門
包裝紙也是
等待你的手
來拆　你不拆
我就聽不到小鹿撞門的
美妙聲響

脣
是人人都有的門
在開與不開間
露出似笑
非笑

究竟蒙娜麗莎
有沒有對達文西露齒微笑
至今仍舊是個謎

有的脣
只為聖杯而開
上了鎖的心
連神都打不開

2015.09.18

玫瑰物語

我們都說
愛玫瑰

我想偷偷
偷偷多愛玫瑰一些些
卻不是花瓶對花的那種愛

其實
我們對玫瑰的愛
並無誰濃誰淡的問題
我們對玫瑰的思念
並無誰多誰少的爭議

你用相機
定格玫瑰的哀愁與美麗
抵抗終將褪色的記憶

我想成為玫瑰的梗
玫瑰的骨
支撐玫瑰笑容

豐腴的　消瘦的
艷麗的　蒼白的
全是玫瑰

跳舞的　恬靜的
著火的　冰霜的
無不是玫瑰

玫瑰有刺
曾挺身抵抗暴力
玫瑰的刺
也會不小心刺傷愛花人
因淌出的血而增色

保證

Promise

花季過後
腦海不斷浮現玫瑰身影
耳畔隨時縈繞玫瑰歌聲
我呼吸玫瑰的體味
我呢喃玫瑰的私語

玫瑰玫瑰
玫瑰不曾消逝
玫瑰是比我更真實的
存在

2015.09.26

風箏

風啊
請把我帶到峰頂
用雲的眼光看風景

請吹我到海上
用落日的單眼看時間

請把我送上彩虹
用上帝的高度看作品

請把我輕輕釋放
讓我用谷底的角度看人間

2015.10.27

曼陀羅 2

畫夢境的曼陀羅課
有人說他從不做夢
有人做著醒不過來的夢
有人做著不願醒來的夢
有人做著莊子的夢
有人做著蝴蝶春夢

無夢的人為別人畫下夢境
在無路可走處
給予
柳暗花明又一春

反覆做惡夢的人
羨慕從不做夢的人
從不做夢的人
羨慕做美夢的人

做美夢的人
遺憾美夢終究要醒轉

畫出毒蛇
釋放恐懼
畫下情人夢
成為一生的詩篇
為他人畫下難忘的夢
彌補自己無夢的缺憾

夢
是現實的一面凹凸鏡
宣稱無夢的人
必定也在清醒地作夢吧

2015.11.09

貓頭鷹

我隱身山邊巢穴
一開窗就迎見台北101
高高的竹節底部
隱藏一隻貓頭鷹

和所有野地貓頭鷹一樣
夜來睜開一雙鑽石般
圓滾滾的眼睛
貓頭鷹具有全身保護色
唯獨疏忽了高調的眼睛

黑色的夜
藏匿我失眠的黑色眼睛
安全感是基本需求

我像是不動聲色的獵人
但面對貓頭鷹

那雙極盡挑逗的眼睛
我恍惚變成
一隻主動獻身的祭物

2015.11.09

海岸

你雙手
圈成我身體的岸
我情感的海洋掀起一片暗潮
浪花不斷淹沒我
不斷奔向堅實海岸

你用文字歌頌不願消退的海洋
你的字和我的字
連結成為鎖鏈般的曲折海岸

多少年後
可能乾涸成為陸地的海洋
將在飽含氧氣的詩句中
永恆地呼吸
和詠嘆

2015.11.16

國旗

我們需要一面旗
一面清清楚楚標誌國家
身分的旗幟

像從母土長出的香蕉葉
愉悅飄揚
在自由的天空下

像母親向你揮別的手
在你遠離故鄉時
仍然伸進夢中搖動思念

像情人風中飄飛的一匹秀髮
在長夜思念中千絲萬縷
繫著兩地牽掛

保證
Promise

國旗自晨霧中誕生
逐漸清晰
燦爛如嬰兒笑容

一面用信仰
希望和愛繪製的國旗
住著國家靈魂

國旗
見證國家苦難
也團結國民成為國家主人

讓國旗
從地平線上升上去
從每一個國民心中升上去

2016.01.20

微電影 2

怕
時間
抹掉你
抹掉你對我濃濃情意

急急投奔你
一路上
路口總豎起
宛如聖母峰的紅燈
　　　命運的紅燈

翻越重重命定
我
又面臨
一片茫茫水域

保證

Promise

我
無舟
又無泳技

若是你
也像我
決心死抱一根浮木
千里相尋

會不會
我們
在水色茫茫中
　　　　彼此錯身
　　　　錯過終身

又或者
終於
我們尋獲彼此

你
卻失落
足以相認的
　　　　共同印記

2016.02.03

月亮的心

你用歌聲
點燃
達卡月光

每當你用華語歌唱
「……月亮代表我的心……」
我恍惚變身一朵夜來香

塞車時
你用歌聲接駁我們
到達音符飛揚的天堂

不塞車時
你用歌聲載我們
飛越海洋和換日線

你華語我英語
恰好留下一個美麗
誤解的空間

即便如此
你仍賣力為我
和你慈父做橋梁

我們和你的
著名詩人父親
溫柔的父親
羅曼蒂克的父親
無所不知的父親
無所不談

我們擊掌歡慶
你瘋狂的父親

保證

Promise

想把受贈的花束
全帶回摩洛哥花瓶綻放
孟加拉花香

我們私自決定
讓你父當我們導遊
米蘭史卡拉歌劇院
是他心中不熄的月亮

福爾摩莎
也有一輪明月
請循著鋪好的銀色月光
隨我追尋島嶼台灣

2016.02.12

在達卡俱樂部摔跤

高跟鞋
不認識俱樂部
在階梯摔跤

夜間
不長眼睛
我在高跟鞋上摔了一跤
撿到一堆關愛眼睛

孟加拉導遊問有沒有受傷
摩洛哥詩人說可以用妮維雅塗抹
台灣詩人說……

從此　我不再怕摔跤
從此　導遊嚴禁我摔跤

保證

Promise

回到台北
結痂傷口
時不時地癢　癢

癢了起來
像埋伏已久的思念

2016.02.12

野柳女王頭 1

全天下都說
妳是女王
其實妳不過是個
女人
愛情是妳的惟一
皇冠

四季
風搶著來密報
他沒來
他
沒來

每一波湧來的潮浪
都帶給妳
他將來
的一線希望

保證

Promise

愛情的女奴
憂傷雙目
穿透層層陰霾
望向
失蹤的愛情

妳得熬過一次
又一次風
寒

別讓咳嗽
咳
斷
妳細弱頸項

妳高貴頸項
早已承受不了

沉重
定情珍珠項鍊

妳卻還在
沒日沒夜尋找
妳那無可取代的
皇冠

2016.03.13

野柳女王頭 2

游離相思海
上岸後
人魚公主
找不到
暗戀的王子

回頭
早已失喪
游回生命海洋的尾巴

從此
擱淺
東方島嶼
成為一則童話

故事尾巴
我和人魚公主沒兩樣

在稱王之前
具有一雙急切尋找
愛情的眼睛
我是她
的分身

2016.03.14

野柳女王頭3

石化身軀
隱藏
一個憂傷的靈
一顆水晶玻璃心

有人欠你　一屁股愛情
有人賒了妳　一輩子眼淚

以口傳耳故事裡
活化的身軀
緩緩走向
各自的祕密花園

未曾許諾的花園
會不會有春天
悄悄萌芽

愛的藤蔓
困在石縫掙扎
終於蔓延
一絲一縷緊緊纏繞我的心

2016.03.14

野柳女王頭 4

如一株植物
私訂終身
在含重鹽地土
歷經多少世紀

捏塑一個世間女子
凝望天涯
風吹　　不動
雨打　　不動
在流言天空下
守候一段浪漫史

或者她像我
只是來海邊靜坐
求一個解脫
因入定太深

變成一個
等待被吻醒的公主

我拋棄找尋
愛情的眼睛
讓滿耳潮浪
日夜為我誦經

2016.03.15

野柳女王頭5

從Modigliani畫布出走的女人

細緻優雅
但哀傷的修長脖子
是Modigliani的夢中情人

一開始畫妳
Modigliani並未給妳
反射情人眸光的眼珠
他說
等到我看見了妳的靈魂
我再把妳的眼珠畫上去

空洞眼眶填滿灰白孤寂
莫名憂傷像一曲月光
遍覆妳無瑕胴體

Modigliani終究
把眼珠賦予妳
形成兩座藍色海洋
激動海浪
一波波溢出妳眼眶

上帝給了妳
尋找光的眼睛
妳卻用眼睛
尋獲苦難愛情

妳手中天秤
愛情重於生命

妳自傷為淌血玫瑰
眼睛還給上帝
靈魂償還愛情

保證

Promise

妳是Modigliani的女人
妳的名字
叫做Jeanne Hébuterne

其實
妳的名字是
女人

2016.03.22

淡水

淡水小鎮
住在蔚藍天空下
依偎綠色海洋

火車運走一節一節舊時光
捷運列車搬來一波一波新人潮

我青春的舞步
曾踩亮淡江大學宮燈大道

馬偕讚嘆過的夕陽
如今在漁人碼頭垂釣
人群如魚聚集

觀音依舊堅持仰臥山頂
迎接你遠道來獻詩

保證

Promise

甚麼是淡水小鎮幸福時光
不是舊時光
不是新時光

從右岸渡到左岸
從花落走向花開
和你並肩走進時間迷宮
將是我此生
最美好時光

2016.04.12

島與海

走在鬧街
感覺自己是一座小小浮島

如果你也是
一座浮島
請和我連結
成為一片景深無限陸地

如果你是一個
神祕海洋
與我有同樣節拍
請用你雙臂
圈成我堅實海岸

每當流淚過多
我感覺自己變成死海

保證

Promise

如果你也是一個海
請和我連結
成為一片汪洋
激起不停舞蹈的浪花

如果你是一座孤島
我請求你住在我的海洋
稀釋我滿懷憂傷
我貝殼的耳朵
要傾聽你
甜蜜耳語

2016.04.15

燭與影 1

幽暗中
你尋求我
以肉身為祭壇
燃燒成為一隻火鳳凰

在你戰慄火花中
我彰顯
成為你
的影子

你愛我有多深
你就燃燒得多激烈
直到吸盡最後一口氧氣

黑暗中我緊緊跟隨你
光的律動
你一吋一吋佔領我

火焰的舞蹈
愛情的舞蹈
終極之美的
死亡雙人舞展

2016.05.07

燭與影 2

源於愛
或恨

不惜
燃燒自己成為一座小火山

不熄
焚燒自己的影子

漫漫長夜
影子是一隻不安的黑蛾

2016.05.08

燭與影 3

你用火光
照亮
我的存在
像一個獨特的舞台

你搖曳火花
像我版圖裡的一支旗幟

我也是被你囚禁的
一個陰影
求助於一陣風

風並未吹熄
你的愛
反而助長你愛的烈焰

淌著淚
你告訴我你正在
一點一滴釋放我

2016.05.14

雕像

被雕刻家吹進一口氣的雕像
擁有許多個不同面向

有些面相眼睛神祕如幽谷
有些面相眼睛燃燒灼灼白焰

有些眼睛渴望濃密睫毛
有些眼睛渴望黑眼珠
有些眼珠渴望淚滴

在永恆的時間裡
我浮躁等待一尊雕像
對我說句真心話

在永恆的等待裡
雕像持續沉醉
在時間的永恆裡

雕像始終沒開口
卻又說盡了一切

我時常為了永恆說了許多
卻終究甚麼都沒說

2016.05.28

我願意

我願意
在深秋為你焚身
給妳紅色的溫暖

但你想要
一整座春天森林

而我只是一株孤獨楓樹

2016.06.30

等

我到橋上
癡癡等你
又過了
一個沒有你的白天

橋在水上
等我
又過了
擁有我的一個夜晚

我在橋上等你好幾年
橋在水上等我好幾個世紀

橋有秋風的嘆息
我有流血的心

2016.07.05

為了……

——《骨折》之17

我每一步
都在靠近你

你迎向一道光
多麼急切
你逃離暴風雨
多麼迫切

你不是這樣的人
是骨折的關係
讓我曲解你

我這麼說
還是
為了靠近你

我寧可逆光
挺進暴風雨
靠近你

2016.08.04

我很想

——《骨折》之19

拄著枴杖
我無法和你玩
捉迷藏

我很想
很想趁你不注意
從背後拍拍你
看你又氣又不敢生氣
但我的枴杖會出聲破壞這詭計

偷偷接近你
是我天大的樂趣
現在我只能戴面具
公然靠向你

2016.08.05

我一再逃避

我一再逃避
你閃電的眼睛
怕閃電之後
眼睛忍不住下雨

我已習慣
讓眼睛每天放晴
這樣
才不會傻傻分不清
是天空讓我下雨
還是我讓天空流淚

在美麗山水中
在多情淡水小鎮裡
在練習擁抱
親吻的詩歌節

保證

Promise

我們原該並肩
走進時間迷宮

在初秋陽光下
在微雨老街中
在美好的時光裡
我反覆練習
離開你

我的一邊是你
一邊是我不斷求助的神

神哪
聽說祢大過人
的困境

2016.09.11

詩人送我一塊石頭

詩人莊金國
送我一塊可愛的石頭
或許幾經輾轉
才到我手中

外形像我熟悉的島嶼
我熱愛的土生土長的土地
一見她
我馬上喊出她的名字
台灣

她像一塊
人見人愛的殖民地
在不同統治者手中
也許被叫過好幾個
不屬於她自己的名字

保證

Promise

若你看到我
卻呼喊她人名字
我必定馬上轉身離去

叫對我的名字
是愛我的第一步

2016.09.12

過敏

腿傷開始發癢
夏秋之交
聽說是一個過敏時節

我在喧嘩聲中
似乎聽到你的耳語
穿過夢的帷幕
我的眼睛似乎看到你微笑
夕陽下有你暖香的觸感
不知名花朵散發你的體香
紅酒似乎從你舌頭游到我舌尖

我的眼睛迴避你
我的心想要忘掉你
你卻顯現一尊神的形象
祢無所不在

保證
Promise

祢佔領我
心的神殿

2016.09.13

作者簡介

陳秀珍，筆名林弦，淡江大學中國文學系畢業。出版有散文集《非日記》（2009年）、詩集《林中弦音》（2010年）和《面具》（2016年）。參加2015年台南福爾摩莎國際詩歌節，2016年孟加拉卡塔克詩高峰會、淡水福爾摩莎國際詩歌節，以及馬其頓奈姆日（Ditët e Naimit）國際詩歌節。

譯者簡介

李魁賢，1937年生，1953年開始發表詩作，曾任台灣筆會會長，國家文化藝術基金會董事長。現任世界詩人運動組織（Movimiento Poetas del Mundo）副會長。詩被譯成各種語文在日本、韓國、加拿大、紐西蘭、荷蘭、南斯拉夫、羅馬尼亞、印度、希臘、美國、西班牙、巴西、蒙古、俄羅斯、古巴、智利、尼加拉瓜、孟加拉等國發表。

出版著作包括《李魁賢詩集》全6冊、《李魁賢文集》全10冊、《李魁賢譯詩集》全8冊、翻譯《歐洲經典詩選》全 25 冊、《名流詩叢》25冊、《人生拼圖——李魁賢回憶錄》，及其他共二百本。英譯詩集有《愛是我的信仰》、《溫柔的美感》、《島與島之間》、《黃昏時刻》和《存在或不存在》。《黃昏時刻》共有英文、蒙古文、羅馬尼亞文、俄文、西班牙文、法文、孟加拉文譯本。

曾獲韓國亞洲詩人貢獻獎、榮後台灣詩獎、賴和文學獎、行政院文化獎、印度麥氏學會詩人獎、吳三連獎新詩獎、台灣新文學貢獻獎、蒙古文化基金會文化名人獎牌和詩人獎章、蒙古建國八百週年成吉思汗金牌、成吉思汗大學金質獎章和蒙古作家聯盟推廣蒙古文學貢獻獎、真理大學台灣文學家牛津獎、韓國高麗文學獎、孟加拉卡塔克文學獎、馬其頓奈姆·弗拉謝里文學獎。

Promise

CONTENTS

*附西班牙語翻譯

Winter II

For welcome the snow

the leaves

leave the vacancy of

whole mountain.

1998

Promise

I promise

I dare to promise

I promise to you with my personality and my life

We promise

We dare to promise

We promise to you with our moral character and our prestige

The party promises to the people

The boss promises to the employee

The merchant promises to the customer

The man promises to the woman

The adult promises to the child

The honeybee promises to the flower

The wave promises to the beach

The wind promises to the leaves

The love promises to the eternity

The God promises to the soul

Promise

Promise

Promise

The bloody history has promised to the peace

1998

The Bird Has Unlimited Freedom

The bird has freedom of unlimited unknown

The bird has freedom of eating without laboring

The bird has freedom of perching without selection

The bird has freedom of singing toward the prison

The bird has freedom of dancing before the master

The bird has freedom of shitting at any place

The bird has freedom of flying to and fro over stormy waves

The bird has freedom of nearsightedness

The bird has freedom of going weak at the legs

The bird has freedom of pecking out wings

The bird has freedom of forgetting love

The bird has freedom of forgetting enemy

Ah, the bird

is free

The bird has freedom of forgetting freedom

1998

Onion

Dissect your heart

drip my tears

a dilemma of love

1998

Reading at Night

As the night curtain
falls all around
I open
the front page
to read a poem
with lip language
silently.

That front page as white
as thoroughly,
I read it thousand times
even ten thousand.

The length of
one poem
as measured is
an entire summer night

completely blue
in liquid state.

The poem
without one word
fulfills dense and numerous sweet
your name.

1998

Reading

You carefully examine a leaf
whether there is an epoch thereon!

The mystery of each leaf vein forwarding to an annual ring
reveals respective prosperous age.

A leaf may lead to visit a forest,
and a forest probably hides
a password to open the world.

You deeply examine
a leaf
as read a Bible respectfully.

2003.12.18

Diving Accident

As I submerged into water,
someone cried for help
someone threw a life buoy
someone jumped into water regardless of danger.
At last, they found
I was simply challenging myself
the extreme limit of diving capability.

When I dropped into water again
someone cheered me going on
someone waited for me with bouquet
no one in the cheer team knew
I was losing my diving ability.

2005.06

The Forest

In autumn, the life's tree,
its memories like leaves
are yellowing and falling
one after another.

Across the forest
the colorful leaves are all around
as if the pages scattered from
the memoires one and another.

Occasionally,
I pick up one leaf
of residue in memory.

The forest stretches endless
I cannot determine which leaf
belongs to which branch.

Some leaves float with the wind
as if the prey struggled on the spider web,
resisting against the strong death.

The path extends far from out of sight
to sometime forgetting to recognize
and eventually towards forgetting to memorize.

In turning round,
the fog engulfs all forest
all memory.

The universe
retrogresses to the beginning of the world.

2013.01.24

People and God I

The people on both sides of the war
believe the same God.

The left side insists——the truth is ours,
The right side insists——the justice is ours.

Both sides face toward the same God at same time
to pray for the victory on the same battlefield.

The God is separated into two halves
and caught in a dilemma.

2014.07.28

People and God II

The people on both sides of the war
believe different Gods.

Both sides face toward own God to pray
for the victory on the same battlefield.

The left side insists own to be victory,
The right side insists opposite to be defeated.

The war between people to people
becomes an innocent war
between God to God.

The people utilizes missiles to decide
whose God
is a real one.

2014.07.28

Bronze Statue I

Even incapable of turning back
the bronze statue erects on
an artificially raised basement
and looks down on the whole world.

After mastication of history
for some tens years,
by now, a little bit residue
of memory cannot be spat out.

The bronze statue with nobody in his eyes
lost himself in the disordered time an space intersection
being in a daze for long years.

Standing on the turning point of history
the bronze statue
is a dementia old man lost his way.

2014.08.14

Bronze Statue II

Tough
competition with mummy
which one would be much more immortal.

The bronze statue compares with mummy
the latter has laid down
the former sustains to stand faintly.

The one provides a soft strength
able to occupy a position
in the famous museum.

The another is
still unable to find out
a place in history.

2014.08.20

Organic Life

You spend your organic life.
First thing as opening your eyes
is going to slide your mobile phone,
sliding to and fro,
slide yourself into an unreal world.

I spend my inorganic life.
First thing as opening my eyes
is going to see you sliding your mobile phone,
sliding to and fro,
slide me out of your organic world.

In the farm of your organic world
are there cocks to wake-up your mind?

You spend your organic life.
I spend my inorganic life.

First thing as opening your eyes
is going to slide your mobile phone,
First thing as opening my eyes
is going to see you sliding your mobile phone.

Sliding to and fro,
you slide yourself into an unreal world.
Sliding to and fro,
you slide me out of your organic world.

In the farm of your organic world
are there cocks to wake-up your mind?

2014.08.05

The Mask

The mask through makeup
can no longer cover the footprints
left behind by trample of the years.

The mask changed by reshaping operation
retrieves the features of youth, yet
the secret of annual rings being concealed within body.

Every one competes to change a face of super star,
the famous doctor busy to reveal for his believers,
changing a face just like exchange a visiting card,
changing a face just like replacing a fig leaf.

However, I have only one face
impossibly returning to my spring time,
fully at easy towards the heaven and the earth,
the features are exhibition stages of natural beauty.

My face loyal to the God

will test

your love to

me.

2014.11.25

Uncertain Scenery

A cloud
drags whole sky
passing through temporal process.

Two eyeballs
lead a concrete body
passing through spatial wilderness.

Overall
would be switched off
by a drunk
red face.

At the moment,
it becomes an uncertain scenery.

2015.03.06

The Sea I

The sea
collects the tears from sky
so that streams the deep blue blood.

The sea
confronts a smiling blue mountain
so that suffers from green lovesick.

Within my heart
there is buried a sea too.

Separated by a sea area
I confront an isolated island
Inaccessible forever.

Whenever I ask the sky
my salty tears

unbearably fall out of my eyes
down to the sea within my heart.

When the sea within my heart floods
I turn to the boundless sea
dripping my pearl tears.

The sea cultivated by tears
will return the tears
to the sky.

2015.07.22

Peach blossom

You said
nobody likes real peach blossom
everybody loves
the plastic flower without tears.

However,
I have been long since
and so far still
beside you.

Your eyes are busy in weeping,
anyway,
without finding me.

2015.07.31

The Heartbeats

A clock was hung on
the heartland of the living room
making a sound of
heartbeats of an old house.

I was absent
in your heartland
yet I desired
to make a sound of your heartbeats.

You occupied
my heart land
but made
a sound of others.

The Son of Man was hung on
the heartland of the history

making a sound of
heartbeat of the rebirth.

2015.08.08

Poetry Recital

The poetry is recited
by means of blooming ears.

I am enchanted by
your mysterious tremolo with a little aroma.
I utilize your poetry
every sentence every word
to tattoo my heart.

I miss the way
within the zigzag labyrinth of your language.
I turn to read a lot of lofty mountains range
at last
I catch the white deer
in the forest among faint cloudy mists with flower scents.

But your footsteps going far away
have disturbed
to hurt my heart.

2015.09.07

The Door

My door
is prepared for you to open.

What secret is hidden under the magician red scarf?
What God resides in the temple?

What hidden behind the door
is an astonished scenery.

The garment
is a thin door,
the wrapping paper too,
waits for your hand
to open, if you do not
I could not hear the sweet sounds
the fawn bumping the door.

The lip
is a door every one has.
It appears
a smiling or not
depending it opens or closed.

After all, it remains a puzzle
whether Mona Lisa showed a grin
to da Vinci.

Some lips
open for Holy Grail,
the locked heart
could not unlocked even by the God.

2015.09.18

Something About Roses

We all say
we love roses

I want to love roses
to love roses a little more in secret
rather than such love that the vase to flowers

In fact
we love roses
without the problem who more and who less
We miss roses
without distribute who more and who less

You use the camera
for rating the sorrow and beauty of the roses
to resist the eventual fading of memories

I want to be the stalk of roses
and the bones of roses
to sustain the smiling of roses

Either chubby or slim
either gorgeous or pale
all are roses

Either in dancing or keeping still
either on fire or under frost
no flowers are not roses

All roses has thorns
insisting to against violence
the thorns of roses may sometime
accidentally stab the flowers-loving people
making the roses more brilliant by their bleeding

保證

Promise

After the blooming season
my mind constantly emerges the figure of roses
my ears at any time resounds the song by roses
I breathe the smell of roses
I mumble the whisper by roses

Roses, oh roses
roses never fade
roses are more real than
my existence

2015.09.26

The Kite

Oh, wind
please bring me to the summit
to watch the landscape with the eyes of cloud,

please blow me to the sea
to watch the time with single eye of sunset,

please send me to the rainbow
to watch the creation at the level of the God,

please release me gently
let me watch the world at the angle from the valley.

2015.10.27

Mandala II

In the lesson for drawing the mandala in dreamland
someone says never dreaming
someone in the dream does not wake up
someone in the dream refuses to wake up
someone fell into the same dream as Zhuangzi did
someone fell into the same dream as the butterfly did

Dreamless people draw dreamland for others
at the place where no way to go
presenting another spring unexpectedly

The people who repeat nightmares
envy the people who never fall into a dream
The people who never fall into a dream
envy the people who has a sweet dream
The people who has a sweet dream
regret eventually wake up from the sweet dream

Drawing a poisonous snake
may release the fear
Drawing a dream to lover
may create poems for a life long
Drawing an unforgettable dream for others
may make up for own deficiency of dreams

The dream
is a meniscus lens of the reality
The people who claim own dreamless
must be in sober dreaming

2015.11.09

Owls

I am secluded in a mountainside domicile
watching Taipei 101 building through opening window
At the bottom of tall bamboo joint
an owl hide there

Like all owls in the wilderness
at night stare its round eyes
like a pair of diamonds
Owls have a full body camouflage
except the high-resolution eyes by neglect

At dark night
I conceal my black eyes due to insomnia
for the basic need of security

I am something like a quiet hunter
but as soon as confronting to a owl

with strong challenging eyes
I become as if
a voluntary sacrifice

2015.11.09

Coast

Your hands embrace as coast
around my body.
My emotional ocean surges from undercurrent,
with waves constantly submerge me,
constantly rushing towards the solid coast.

You praise by words the ocean reluctant to subside,
your words and my words
link to become the meandering coast.

Many years afterwards,
the ocean probably becoming as dry land
will perpetually breathe
and chant
in the poetry sentences impregnated with oxygen.

2015.11.16

National Flag

We need a flag,
a flag clearly indicating
our national identity.

The banana leaves grown from motherland
pleasantly fluttering
under the sky of freedom.

Like mother's waving hands
extending into your dream to vibrate your mind
after your leaving homeland.

Like the lover's long hairs dancing with the wind,
tying the longing for each other in a distance
with thousands of concerns at long nights.

A national flag will be born from morning frog
gradually vivid clarified
and brilliant like the baby smile.

The national flag
will witness the suffering of a state to be born
and solidify the nationals as the masters of country.

Let the national flag
arises from the horizon
from the soul of each national.

2016.01.20

Micro Movie II

I was afraid
time
will erase you
erase your deep affection for me

I run hurriedly to you
along the way
the junction was always erected
a red light as if the Mount Everest
    the red light of fate

Overrunning the heavy destiny
I
further confront
a vast expanse of water

保證

Promise

I have

neither boat

nor swimming skills

If you were the

same as me too

decided to hold a driftwood insistently

to encounter together for thousand miles distance

whether

we will probably

in the vast water

  passed a wrong way

  and missed each other for life

otherwise

at last

we found each other

but you

have lost

any common mark

sufficiently to be recognized

2016.02.03

The Heart of Moon

——To Zakariae Bouhmala

Your song
switches on
the moonlight in Dhaka.

Whenever you sing in Mandarin
"… …the moon represents my heart… …"
I turn myself into a tuberose.

Whenever the traffic jam
you connect us with your song
to a paradise fulfilled with melody.

Whenever the traffic smooth
you bring us with your song
flying over the ocean and the date line.

Your Chinese and my English
just leave a beautiful
misunderstood space.

Even so
you still endeavor to serve as a bridge
between me and your father.

We both and your
father, a famous poet,
a gentle father,
a romantic father,
an intellectual father,
talk about everything.

We slapped high fives in celebration
for your crazy father

thinking about to bring the bouquets
dedicated in Bangladesh back to Morocco
for emitting the fragrance in the vase.

We decided at our will
asking your father as our guide
to Milan Scala Opera House,
the moon never distinguished in his mind.

In Formosa
there is also moon,
please follow the paved silver moonlight
accompany me to pursue with Taiwan island.

2016.02.12

Falling in Dhaka Club

My high heels,
unfamiliar with the club,
fell down on the steps.

At night,
due to inattention,
I fell with my heels,
whereupon picked up a lot of careful eyes.

Bangla tour guide concerned about any hurt,
Moroccan poet suggested to rub some Nivea
Taiwan poet said ......

Since then, I am no longer afraid of falling
Since then, the guide prohibited me from falling

After returned to Taipei
the wound was healed
but itches itch from time to time

It itches
something like long buried yearning.

2016.02.12

Queen's Head Rock in Yehliu Geopark I

You are the Queen
everyone all over the world says so
In fact, you are nothing but
a woman
the Love is the only one crown
of yours

At all seasons
the rushing wind always gives you this secret:
he is not coming
he is
not coming

Every surging tidal wave
brings you a ray of hope
that he
will be coming

You as a slave of love

looks sadly with eyes

penetrating through layers of haze

toward

the lost love

You must withstand

again and again wind

cold

Don't let cough

coughs to

broken

your slim and faint neck

Your noble neck

has long since been intolerable to

heavy pearl necklace
as a token of love

Yet you are still
day and night looking for
your unique
crown

2016.03.13

Queen's Head Rock in Yehliu Geopark II

After landing
from love yearning sea
the mermaid
failed to find the prince
that she loves in secret

As soon as looking back
she has lost her tail
for swimming back to the ocean of life

Since then
she beached on
an oriental island
becoming a fairy tale

At the end of this tale
I am not different from the mermaid

Before declaring by myself as a Queen

I have the eager eyes to look

for love

I am her

incarnation

2016.03.14

Queen's Head Rock in Yehliu Geopark III

This fossil body
conceals
a sad soul
a crystal glass heart

Someone owes you a lot of loves
Someone gives you a credit for life long tears

In oral legend
the life-giving body
went slowly
towards respective secret garden

In the never promised garden
would the spring sprouts
silently

The vine of love
has been trapped in struggle within the stony gaps
and eventually creeps
little by little around my heart tightly

2016.03.14

Queen's Head Rock in Yehliu Geopark IV

Like a plant
engaged in secret
to the heavy salty land
for centuries

Someone molded a living woman
looking out over the world
unmoved in wind blowing
unmoved in rain beating
to wait for a romantic story
under the rumor sky

May be she like me
just coming here to sit quietly
for seeking a relief
but meditating too deep

to become
a princess to be awaken by a kiss

I closed my eyes to look for love
rather let sound wave full-loaded in the ears
chanting the sutras for me day and night

2016.03.15

Queen's Head Rock in Yehliu Geopark V

You are the woman emerging from the canvas of Modigliani

With a slim and elegant
but sorrowful long neck
you are the beloved of Modigliani in dream

At the very beginning to paint you
Modigliani didn't give you the eyeballs to
reflect the shine of lover's eyes

The empty eye sockets are full of gray loneliness
with unknown sadness like a song of moonlight
covering all over your pure body

Modigliani has eventually
endowed the eyeballs to you
forming two blue oceans

with excited waves one after another
overflowing your eye sockets

The God gave you
the eyes looking for light
but you use your eyes
to find out bitter love

In the balance on your hand
the love is heavier than the life

You hurt yourself as a bloody rose
returned your eyes to the God
and the soul to compensate the love

You are the woman belonging to Modigliani
Your name is Jeanne Hébuterne

In fact

you are just named

a woman

2016.03.22

Tamsui

Under the blue sky
Tamsui the township
nestles among the green ocean.

The train transported away the old time a little by little.
The MRT* brings in the flocks of tourists in waves.

My youth dance steps have polished
the lanterns avenue in Tamkang University.

The sunset admired by Rev. Mackay**
now fishes by the Fisherman's Wharf.
The tourists flock as fishes.

Guanyin*** has been insisting to lay on the mountaintop
in greeting you from a distance to dedicate poetry.

What is the happy time in Tamsui
is neither the old time
nor the new age.

From right bank to the left,
from flowers withering to blooming,
I accompany with you side by side into a time labyrinth,
in this way to keep the best time
surely in all my life.

* MRT is abbreviated from Mass Rapid Transit, the metro system in Taipei area.
** Rev. George Leslie Mackay (1844~1901) was the first Canadian Presbyterian missionary to Formosa on 1871 New Year's Eve and then have lived in Tamsui all his life.
***Guanyin, the Bodhisattva of Compassion or Goddess of Mercy (Sanskrit Avalokiteśvara).

2016.04.12

Island and Sea

Walking along the downtown street
I feel myself as a small floating island.

If you are also
a floating island,
please connect with me
to become a land with unlimited scenery.

If you are
a mysterious ocean
having same beats as mine,
please embrace my solid coast
with your arms.

Whenever weeping too much
I feel myself becoming a dead sea.

保證

Promise

If you are also a sea
please connect with me
to become a vast expanse of waters
swashing waves in dance ceaselessly.

If you are an isolated island
I invite you to reside within my ocean
to reduce my full sadness.
My ears of seashells
will listen to your
sweet whispers.

2016.04.15

Candle and Shadow I

In the darkness
you are looking for me
to have my body as an altar
burn into a firing phoenix.

In your trembling spark
I manifest myself
and become
your shadow.

By how much you love me
you will burn how intensively
until the last oxygen extinguished.

In the darkness I follow you step by step
while you occupy me inch by inch
with a rhythm of the light.

保證

Promise

The dance of flame
and the dance of love
play a twin dance show of death
with an ultimate beautiful.

2016.05.07

Candle and Shadow II

Whether it originates from
either love or hate.

You don't hesitate to burn yourself
becoming a small volcano

and to incinerate
your shadow ceaselessly.

In the long night
the shadow is an unstable black moth.

2016.05.08

Candle and Shadow III

By light
you illuminate
my existence
like an unique stage.

You sway the flickers
like a flag in my territory.

Prisoned by you
I am also a shadow
to have recourse to a gust of wind.

The wind would not
blow out your love
instead promoting your flame of love.

In tears

you are telling me

to release me a little by little.

2016.05.14

The Sculpture

The sculpture carefully crafted by the sculptor
displays various different aspects.

In some aspects its eyes are as mysterious as secluded valley.
In some aspects its eyes are as shining as white flame.

Some eyes long for dense eyelashes.
Some eyes long for black eyeballs.
Some eyes long for tear drops.

In the everlasting time
I wait impatiently for one statue
saying one true word to me.

During the perpetual waiting
the sculpture continuously addicts to
the temporal eternity.

The sculpture keeps silent,
yet speaks out everything.

I always say much for pursuing eternity,
yet nothing after all.

2016.05.28

I Will

I will
burn myself in late autumn
providing you a reddish warm

But you rather want
a whole forest in spring time

while I am just a maple tree alone

2016.06.30

Waiting

I have waited for you
on the bridge
for another whole day
without finding you.

The bridge has waited for me
on the water
for another whole night
with holding me.

I have waited for you
on the bridge for years,
the bridge has waited for me
on the water for centuries.

The bridge sighs with an autumn wind,
I bleed out of my heart.

2016.07.05

For the Purpose of......

—No. 17 from "Bone Fracture"

I am approaching to you
by every step.

How urgently
you run toward a streak of light.
How quickly
you escape from the storm.

You are not such a person,
simply because my bone fracture
makes me misunderstanding you.

I say so, anyway,
for the purpose of
approaching to you.

I would rather
backwards the light
advancing into the storm
approaching to you.

2016.08.04

I Really Want

Hobbling along on crutches
I cannot play with you
Hide-and-seek.

I really want
pat you from behind
as you pay no attention,
to see you at once losing temper and daring not angry,
this trick ineffective due to the sounding of my crutches.

Approaching to you in secret
is my utmost fun.
At the moment I simply wear a mask
leaning against you in public.

2016.08.05

I Escape Over and Over

I escape over and over
from your lightning eyes,
worrying about your eyes unable
to restrain from raining, after lightning

I am used to
allow my eyes clear up everyday,
in such
would not unable to distinguish between
whether the sky makes me raining
or I make the sky weeping.

In the beautiful landscapes,
in the affectionate town Tamsui,
during the poetry festival
in practice of hug and kiss for greeting,

we should be walking side by side
into the temporal labyrinth.

Under the autumn sunshine,
on the light rainy old street,
in the pleasant season
I practice over and over
leaving you.

At my one side are you and
other side is the God I pray for help.

Oh, my God,
it is said your plight
more serious than human being.

2016.09.11

The Poet Presented to me a Stone

The poet Chuang Chin-kuo
Presented to me a lovely stone,
arriving at my hands
probably transferred over and over.

Its profile assimilated with my familiar island,
my beloved native land.
As soon as I saw it
I immediately call out its name
Taiwan.

It looks like
a colony beloved by all,
under different rulers
called several names,
none belonging to itself.

保證

Promise

When you encounter with me,
call me other names,
I definitely turn away at once.

Calling me my exact name
is the first step to love me.

2016.09.12

Allergy

The wound on my leg started itching.
It is said a allergy period
when summer turns to autumn.

Among the clamor
seems hearing your whisper,
passing through the curtain of dream
seems seeing your smile.
There is your warm touch at sunset,
your fragrance radiated from unknown flower,
the wine streams from your tongue to my tongue tip.

My sight avoids you,
my mind wants to forget you,
rather you appear as a figure of the God.
You are everywhere.

保證

Promise

You occupy
the temple within my heart.

2016.09.13

About the Author

Chen Hsiu-chen, alias Chen Xiu-zhen and Lin Hsien, graduated from Department of Chinese Literature in Tamkang University and has been served as an editor in newspaper and magazines. Her publications include prose "*A Diary About My Son*" (2009), poetry "*String Echo in Forest*" (2010) and "*Mask*" (2016). She participated 2015 Formosa International Poetry Festival in Tainan, Taiwan, 2016 Kathak International Poets Summit in Dhaka, Bangladesh, 2016 Formosa International Poetry Festival in Tamsui, Taiwan, and 2016 International Poetry Festival "Ditët e Naimit" in Tetova, Macedonia.

About the Translator

Lee Kuei-shien (b. 1937) began to write poems in 1953, was elected as President of Taiwan P.E.N., and served as chairman of National Culture and Arts Foundation. At present he is the Vice President of Movimiento Poetas del Mundo. His poems have been translated and published in Japan, Korea, Canada, New Zealand, Netherlands, Yugoslavia, Romania, India, Greece, USA, Spain, Brazil, Mongolia, Russia, Cuba, Chile, Nicaragua and Bangladesh.

Published works include "*Collected Poems*" in six volumes, "*Collected Essays*" in ten volumes, "*Translated Poems*" in eight volumes, "*Anthology of European Poetry*" in 25 volumes and "*Elite Poetry Series*" in 25 volumes, "*Jigsaw Puzzle of Life——memoir of Lee Kuei-shien*" and others about 200 books in total. His poems in English translation editions include "*Love is my Faith*", "*Beauty of Tenderness*", "*Between Islands*", "*The Hour of Twilight*" and "*Existence or Non-Existence*". The book "*The Hour of Twilight*" has been translated into

English, Mongol, Romanian, Russian, Spanish, French, Korean and Bengali and Albanian languages.

Awarded with Merit of Asian Poet, Korea, Rong-hou Taiwanese Poet Prize, Lai Ho Literature Prize and Premier Culture Prize. He also received the Michael Madhusudan Poet Award, Wu San-lien Prize in Literature, Poet Medal from Mongolian Cultural Foundation, Chinggis Khaan Golden Medal for 800 Anniversary of Mongolian State, Oxford Award for Taiwan Writers, Prize of Corea Literature of Korea, Kathak Literary Award of Bangladesh and Literary Prize "Naim Frashëri" of Macedonia.

Promesa

CONTENIDO

Invierno II

Para dar la bienvenida a la nieve,
las hojas
dejan espacio

a toda la montaña.

1998

Promesa

Prometo.

Me atrevo a prometer.

Prometo sobre mi persona y mi vida.

Nosotros prometemos.

Nos atrevemos a prometer.

Le prometemos sobre nuestra moralidad y nuestro prestigio.

El partido promete al pueblo.

El jefe promete al empleado.

El vendedor promete al cliente.

El hombre promete a la mujer.

El adulto promete al niño.

La abeja promete a la flor.

La ola promete a la playa.

El viento promete a la hoja.

El amor promete a la eternidad.

Dios promete al alma.

Promesas.

Promesas.

Promesas.

La sangrienta historia promete la paz.

1998

Cebolla

Cruza tu corazón,

fluyen mis lágrimas,

rompecabezas del amor.

1998

Buceo

Me hundo en el agua.
Alguien grita pidiendo ayuda.
Alguien trae con un salvavidas.
Algunas personas se precipitan al agua.
Finalmente, me encontraron.
Acabo de retarme a mí mismo
probando los límites de mi buceo.

Cuando caí en el agua otra vez
algunas personas me animaban.
Algunas me esperaban con flores.
Aquellos que me animaban no sabían
que poco a poco había olvidado cómo bucear.

2005.06

Hombre y Dios I

Ambos bandos en guerra
creen en el mismo Dios.

De pie, los de la izquierda creen en su propia verdad,
y a la derecha están aquellos convencidos de su propia justicia.

Ambos lados opuestos ante el mismo Dios,
orando por la victoria en el mismo campo de batalla.

Dios, dividido en dos mitades,
es un dilema.

2014.07.28

Hombre y Dios II

Ambos bandos en guerra
creen en dioses diferentes.

Cada uno ruega a su Dios
por la victoria en la batalla.

Convencida la izquierda de alcanzar la victoria.
Convencida la derecha de que la otra parte perderá.

La guerra entre hombres se convierte
en una guerra entre Dioses
inocentes.

Los hombres deciden quién es
el verdadero Dios
recurriendo a cañones de artillería.

2014.07.28

Estatua de Bronce I

Sin poder retroceder hacia ninguna parte
la estatua se mantiene en pie.
Sobre un duro pedestal creado por el hombre:
la arrogancia del mundo.

Mastica
décadas de historia.
Ahora.
Sin salivar ni un residuo de memoria.

Estatua desafiante.
Perdida en una intersección de tiempo deformado,
¿cuánto tiempo hace que sueña?

Desde el instante en que decide el curso de la historia,
la estatua de bronce
se parece a un demente que no pudiera encontrar su camino.

2014.07.28

Estatua de Bronce II

Dureza.
La estatua juega con la momia,
¿quién es más inmortal?

La estatua de bronce y la momia.
Una yace acostada.
La otra se mantiene en pie obstinadamente.

Una posee un poder blando
y tiene una plaza
en el Museo.

La otra
todavía no ha encontrado su lugar
en la historia.

2014.08.20

Paisaje incierto

Una nube
arrastrando el cielo entero,
¿cuánto tiempo ha recorrido?

Dos ojos
dirigiendo el cuerpo,
¿cuántos desiertos han recorrido?

Todo esto
está a punto de ser
un rostro difuso,
unas luces apagadas.

Se convirtió en un paisaje incierto
en un instante.

2015.03.06

Mar I

Mar.
Recoge las lágrimas del cielo,
fluyendo con sangre azul.

Mar.
Mira a una montaña, sonriendo mutuamente a la distancia
y, por ello, infectados ambos, mar y montaña, de verde añoranza.

En mi corazón
también hay un océano oculto.

Aislado por el mar lejano,
una isla inaccesible y yo
nos miramos mutuamente.

Cada vez que yo miraba al cielo,
mis ojos no podían evitar

derramar las lágrimas saladas
del corazón.

Cuando se inundó el océano del corazón,
me volví hacia el océano y
cayeron mis lágrimas como perlas.

El océano regado de lágrimas
las devolverá algún día
a los cielos.

2015.07.22

Recital

Con oídos florecientes
recitar poesía.

Me fascinaba
en tu trino misterioso y ebrio
tu poema,
cada frase y palabra
quedaron grabadas en mi corazón.

Me he perdido
en el tortuoso laberinto de tu lenguaje.
Trepé numerosas montañas.
Finalmente
capturé el ciervo blanco
en un bosque de niebla, en la delicada fragancia de las flores.

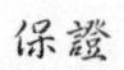

Promesa

Pero me perturban tus pasos alejándose,

percuten en mi corazón.

2015.09.07

Puerta

Mi puerta
para permitir que la abras.

¿Cuál es el secreto oculto bajo el mantel rojo del mago?
¿Qué Dios vive en el templo?

Se esconde detrás de la puerta
un escenario hecho para hacerte exclamar.

Ropa
es una capa delgada de puerta.
También papel de embalaje
esperando que tus manos
lo abran.　Si tú no lo abres
no podré escuchar el maravilloso latido de un corazón acelerado.

Los labios
son las puertas que posee cada uno,
donde aparece la sonrisa misteriosa
entre la puerta abierta y la cerrada.

La Mona Lisa
¿le dio su sonrisa a Da Vinci?
Sigue siendo un enigma.

Algunos labios
se abren sólo por el Santo Grial.
El corazón cerrado
ni siquiera Dios puede abrirlo.

2015.09.18

Una historia de Rosa

Todos decimos
amar las rosas.

Me gustaría
amar las rosas un poco más en secreto,
pero no con el tipo de amor del jarrón de flores.

De hecho,
nadie sabe en quién alienta con más fuerza
el amor por las rosas.

Utilizas la cámara
para congelar la tristeza y la belleza de la rosa,
para resistir el desvanecimiento de la memoria.
Quiero ser un tallo de rosa,
un hueso de rosa,
un soporte para la sonrisa de la rosa.

Las rechonchas, las delgadas
las brillantes, las pálidas,
todas son rosas.

El baile, el sosiego,
el hielo y el fuego,
todos son rosas.

Las rosas tienen espinas
para resistir a la violencia.
Las espinas de las rosas
también apuñalan accidentalmente a sus amantes,
y se enriquecen con la sangre.

Después de la época de floración
pienso a menudo en las rosas. El canto de las rosas permanece en mis
oídos.

Respiro su fragancia.

Susurro los susurros de las rosas.

Rosas, rosas.

Nunca se desvanecen las rosas.

Las rosas son más reales que mi

existencia.

2015.09.26

Mandala II

En la clase de dibujo, un Mandala.
Algunos dicen que nunca han soñado.
Algunas personas se despiertan con sueño.
Alguien está soñando que no quiere despertar.
Algunas personas sueñan con el filósofo Zhuangzi.
Alguien está soñando con una mariposa.

Los otros, sin sueños, dibujan sueños para otros.
Cuando no hay salida
dar
otra vista de primavera.

Las personas con pesadillas repetitivas
envidian a las personas que nunca sueñan.
Las que nunca sueñan
envidian a las personas que tienen sueños dulces.

Las personas con sueños dulces
desafortunadamente tienen que despertar al final.

Con dibujos de serpientes
se libera el miedo.
Dibujando al amante soñado
la vida se convierte en un poema.
Para salvar y compensar su falta de sueños
pintaban los sueños inolvidables de otros.

Soñar
es un espejo convexo y cóncavo de la realidad.
Se supone que las personas sin sueños
en lo profundo también sueñan.

2015.11.09

Búho

Oculto en la guarida de la ladera.
Con una ventana abierta recibe al "Taipei 101".
En el fondo del alto bambú
se oculta un búho.

Al igual que los otros búhos salvajes,
cuando llega la noche abre, como un par de diamantes,
sus ojos saltones.
El búho posee un sistema de camuflaje,
que acaba en el alto perfil de los ojos.

En la negra noche
se esconden mis ojos insomnes.
Una sensación de seguridad es el requisito básico.

Soy como un cazador en silencio.
Pero frente a los ojos

provocativos del búho,

con gusto me hubiera convertido en su presa.

2015.11.09

Orilla

Sus manos,
círculos, me abrazan convirtiendo en orilla mi cuerpo.
Una resaca nace en el océano de mis emociones.
Me veo constantemente inundada por las olas hacia la costa sólida.

Con las letras tú cantas el océano no calmado.
Tu palabra y mi palabra se unieron como un eslabón en la cadena en
la costa tortuosa.

Años más tarde aunque el océano se convierta en una tierra seca,
aún respirará eternamente.
En los versos llenos de aire.
En el canto.

2015.11.16

La bandera nacional

Necesitamos una bandera.
Una que refleje claramente a la nación.
Un estandarte de identidad.

Al igual que las hojas de plátano que cultiva la Madre Tierra,
volando placenteramente
bajo el cielo libre.

Como la mano derecha de la madre, que se agita despidiéndote,
y todavía se sacude con añoranza en su sueño
cuando te encuentras lejos de casa.

Innumerables pensamientos en la noche
como los cabellos de un amante en el viento,
atando dos lugares.

La bandera que nació de la niebla en la madrugada
es cada vez más clara y
brillante, como la sonrisa de un bebé.

Es la bandera que se dibuja con la fe,
la esperanza y el amor,
donde vive el alma del país.

La bandera
es el testigo del sufrimiento del país,
uniendo a la población para convertirse en su propia dueña.

Que la bandera
se ice desde la línea de horizonte,
elevándose desde la mente de cada ciudadano.

2016.01.20

Cortometraje II

Me da miedo que

el tiempo

te borre.

Borre tu afecto profundo hacia mí.

Me entrego a ti con toda prisa.

En el camino

se encuentran la luz roja como el Everest

en las intersecciones.

La luz roja del destino.

Cruzando numerosos destinos

yo

de nuevo estoy frente a

un océano inmenso sin límites

Yo

no tengo barco

ni sé cómo nadar.

Si,

al igual que yo,

con determinación te aferras a una madera a la deriva,

se acabará el camino para encontrarnos.

¿No vamos a

perdernos

en el vasto océano de color?

¿A perder toda la vida?

O,

finalmente,

nos encontraremos el uno al otro.

Pero tú
perdiste el rastro compartido
con que reconocernos.

2016.02.03

Quisiera

Yo quisiera
quemarme por ti en otoño
para darte un cálido color rojo.

Pero tú quieres
un bosque de primavera.

Y yo soy sólo un arce solitario.

2016.06.30

Esperar

Fui al puente,

a esperarte

y otra vez

un día sin ti.

El puente me espera

sobre el agua

y otra vez

seré tuya una noche entera.

En el puente yo te esperé muchos años,

el puente sobre el agua me esperó muchos siglos.

El puente posee un suspiro otoñal,

y yo tengo un corazón sangrante.

2016.07.05

Poetisa

Chen Hsiu-chen, pseudónimo de Chen Xiu-zhen o Lin Hsien. Se graduó en literatura china por el Departamento de Chino de la Universidad Tamkang, Taiwán. Ha sido editora de periódicos y revistas. Ha publicado el ensayo "A Diary About My Son" (2009) y los poemarios "String Echo in Forest" (2010) y "Mask" (2016). Ha participado en los siguientes festivales de poesía: Festival Internacional de Poesía de Formosa en Tainan (Taiwán, 2015), Cumbre Internacional Kathak de Poetas en Dhaka (Bangladesh, 2016), Festival Internacional de Poesía de Formosa en Tamsui, (Taiwán, 2016) y Festival Internacional de Poesía "Ditët e Naimit" en Tetova, (Macedonia, 2016).

Traductora

Chien Jui-ling , pseudónimo de Nuria Jean. Secretaria de la Facultad de Lenguas Extranjeras de la Universidad Providence, Taiwán. Profesora a tiempo parcial del Departamento de Inglés Aplicado y Centro de Educación Continua, Overseas Chinese University, Taiwán.

簡瑞玲，靜宜大學外語學院秘書，兼任僑光科技大學應用英語系、推廣教育中心講師。

語言文學類　PG1751　台灣詩叢02

保證 Promise · Promesa
——陳秀珍漢英西三語詩集

作　　者 / 陳秀珍（Chen Hsiu-chen）
英語譯者 / 李魁賢（Lee Kuei-shien）
西語譯者 / 簡瑞玲（Chien Jui-ling）
叢書策劃 / 李魁賢（Lee Kuei-shien）
責任編輯 / 林昕平
圖文排版 / 周妤靜
封面設計 / 葉力安

發 行 人 / 宋政坤
法律顧問 / 毛國樑　律師
出版發行 / 秀威資訊科技股份有限公司
114台北市內湖區瑞光路76巷65號1樓
電話：+886-2-2796-3638　傳真：+886-2-2796-1377
http://www.showwe.com.tw
劃撥帳號 / 19563868　戶名：秀威資訊科技股份有限公司
讀者服務信箱：service@showwe.com.tw
展售門市 / 國家書店（松江門市）
104台北市中山區松江路209號1樓
電話：+886-2-2518-0207　傳真：+886-2-2518-0778
網路訂購 / 秀威網路書店：http://www.bodbooks.com.tw
國家網路書店：http://www.govbooks.com.tw

2017年4月　BOD一版
定價：280元

國家圖書館出版品預行編目

保證 Promise・Promesa : 陳秀珍漢英西三語詩集 /
陳秀珍著 ; 李魁賢英譯 ; 簡瑞玲西譯. -- 一版.
-- 臺北市 : 秀威資訊科技, 2017.04
面 ;　公分. -- (臺灣詩叢 ; 2)
BOD版
ISBN 978-986-326-415-6(平裝)

851.486　　106003584

讀者回函卡

感謝您購買本書，為提升服務品質，請填妥以下資料，將讀者回函卡直接寄回或傳真本公司，收到您的寶貴意見後，我們會收藏記錄及檢討，謝謝！

如您需要了解本公司最新出版書目、購書優惠或企劃活動，歡迎您上網查詢或下載相關資料：http:// www.showwe.com.tw

您購買的書名：＿＿＿＿＿＿＿＿＿＿＿＿＿＿＿＿＿＿＿＿

出生日期：＿＿＿＿年＿＿＿＿月＿＿＿＿日

學歷：□高中（含）以下　□大專　□研究所（含）以上

職業：□製造業　□金融業　□資訊業　□軍警　□傳播業　□自由業

□服務業　□公務員　□教職　□學生　□家管　□其它＿＿＿

購書地點：□網路書店　□實體書店　□書展　□郵購　□贈閱　□其他

您從何得知本書的消息？

□網路書店　□實體書店　□網路搜尋　□電子報　□書訊　□雜誌

□傳播媒體　□親友推薦　□網站推薦　□部落格　□其他＿＿＿＿

您對本書的評價：（請填代號　1.非常滿意　2.滿意　3.尚可　4.再改進）

封面設計＿＿　版面編排＿＿　內容＿＿　文／譯筆＿＿　價格＿＿

讀完書後您覺得：

□很有收穫　□有收穫　□收穫不多　□沒收穫

對我們的建議：＿＿＿＿＿＿＿＿＿＿＿＿＿＿＿＿＿＿＿＿

＿＿＿＿＿＿＿＿＿＿＿＿＿＿＿＿＿＿＿＿＿＿＿＿＿＿

＿＿＿＿＿＿＿＿＿＿＿＿＿＿＿＿＿＿＿＿＿＿＿＿＿＿

＿＿＿＿＿＿＿＿＿＿＿＿＿＿＿＿＿＿＿＿＿＿＿＿＿＿

請貼
郵票

11466
台北市內湖區瑞光路 76 巷 65 號 1 樓
秀威資訊科技股份有限公司 收
BOD 數位出版事業部

（請沿線對折寄回，謝謝！）

姓　　名：＿＿＿＿＿＿＿＿ 年齡：＿＿＿＿ 性別：□女　□男

郵遞區號：□□□□□

地　　址：＿＿＿＿＿＿＿＿＿＿＿＿＿＿＿＿

聯絡電話：(日)＿＿＿＿＿＿＿＿＿ (夜)＿＿＿＿＿＿＿＿＿

E-mail：＿＿＿＿＿＿＿＿＿＿＿＿＿＿＿＿